THE LIAR'S INN

Rachel McLean writes thrillers that make your pulse race and your brain tick. Originally a self-publishing sensation, she has sold millions of copies digitally, with massive success in the UK, and a growing reach internationally. She is the author of the Dorset Crime novels and the spin-off McBride & Tanner series and Cumbria Crime series. In 2021, she won the Kindle Storyteller Award with *The Corfe Castle Murders* and her books regularly hit No1 in the Bookstat ebook chart on launch.

Joel Hames is a Lancashire-based writer of crime fiction, and the editor of million-selling books across multiple genres. Joel's own works include the Dead North series featuring lawyer Sam Williams, and the psychological thriller *The Lies I Tell*. Most recently, he has been working with titan of crime fiction Rachel McLean on the hugely successful Cumbria Crime series.

ALSO BY RACHEL MCLEAN AND JOEL HAMES

Cumbria Crime series

The Harbour
The Mine
The Cairn
The Barn
The Lake
The Wood
...and more to come

RACHEL McLEAN & JOEL HAMES

CUMBRIA CRIME NOVELLA

THE LIAR'S INN

ACKROYD PUBLISHING

Copyright © 2024 by Rachel McLean and Joel Hames

All rights reserved.

No part of this book may be reproduced in any form or by any electronic or mechanical means, including information storage and retrieval systems, without written permission from the author, except for the use of brief quotations in a book review.

This is a work of fiction. Names, characters, businesses, places, events and incidents are either the products of the author's imagination or used in a fictitious manner. Any resemblance to actual persons, living or dead, or actual events is purely coincidental.

Ackroyd Publishing

ackroydpublishing.com

Printed and bound in the UK by CPI Group (Uk) Ltd, Croydon CR0 4YY

THE LIAR'S INN

CHAPTER ONE

"You taking part?"

DI Carl Whaley turned towards the voice. Tall, lean, white hair to his shoulders: the man would have been a dead ringer for an Old Testament prophet if it weren't for the green stain of mushy peas on his teeth.

"I'm sorry?" Carl said.

"You. You look like you could spin a yarn or two." The man pointed towards the makeshift stage, where a microphone awaited the next contestant. "Not one of them politicians, are you?"

His partner, DI Zoe Finch, laughed. "He's not taking part, and he's not a politician, either. A good thing, on both counts, as far as I'm concerned."

Besides, when it came to the World's Biggest Liar competition, politicians were banned. It was supposed to be an amateur event, after all. Zoe and Carl had been joking about it just a few minutes earlier as they tucked into the tatie pot stew that was a traditional feature of the event. She'd told him the Professional Standards Division of Cumbria Police should be banned for the same reasons. He'd pretended to be offended, but hadn't managed to keep it up for long.

PSD might be cloak and dagger, but if there was one thing Carl wasn't, it was the World's Biggest Liar. Zoe and Carl had secrets from each other, but those were professional secrets, not personal ones. And if she didn't know what Carl's secrets were, at least she knew why he kept them. PSD and CID couldn't tell each other everything.

For the time being, things between them seemed to be working.

The murmur around the room dropped as Stu Cosby marched onto the stage. He grabbed the microphone like the seasoned performer he was, and took up position in front of the screen where the name of the event had been briefly displayed, before a technical problem had turned it dark. Zoe had read up about the event and knew Cosby was a regular, a runner-up in the past, and, apparently, a traditionalist, whatever that meant.

She listened in silence as he regaled the crowded function room with tales of the secret supervillain's lair located beneath the surface of nearby Wastwater. His accent was strong and some of the dialect was new to Zoe, but she'd been in Cumbria long enough to pick up the general sense.

There were a few laughs as Cosby strode about the stage, insisting it was all true and he had the evidence to prove it. But from her spot near the front, Zoe could see the frustration on his face. The crowd was restless, people coming and going while he spoke, whispers at the back. His tale was too wild, too impersonal, and there wasn't enough of Cosby's own life in it – real or fictional – to make it stand out.

Cosby thanked them and edged into the crowd, and then Izzie Hopkirk took to the stage.

If politicians were banned, and lawyers had been until recently, women were hardly encouraged. A female comedian had won the event nearly twenty years earlier, but since then, there had been precious little representation from the women of Cumbria. Zoe was keen to see how Izzie would perform.

Izzie Hopkirk was a tall woman in her early forties, with short, spiky brown hair, and an engaging smile that started nervous, but broadened as she sensed the crowd warming to her theme. Unlike Cosby, she kept to the same spot throughout her monologue.

"The thing is," Izzie was saying, her voice lowered as if imparting serious, confidential information, "it's always been something I've been obsessed with, you know? As long as I can remember, I used to dream about the Beast of Cumbria. Because, unlike the rest of you, I've seen it."

Nobody was talking now. Zoe sensed movement at the back of the room and turned to see a man push his way in from the main bar, past the forlorn figure of Stu Cosby. But apart from the rustle of people edging out of each other's way, there was absolute silence.

"But that's not the thing," Izzie continued. "I mean, I know I've seen her, and the husband believes me, but he'll believe anything I say. But you lot? You're experts, you are. You probably wouldn't believe me if I dragged the thing in here on a lead."

Laughter. She went on. "What I'm here to tell you – and keep it to yourselves," she added, her voice dropping to almost a whisper, "is what I've done about it."

She paused, and Zoe glanced around the room.

Every head was turned towards the stage. There was a woman a few seats away, her hair piled messily on the top of her head, who was scowling as Izzie spoke, but everyone else was captivated. Izzie Hopkirk was a natural.

"Me and my husband have been saving for a bigger house," Izzie said, her voice relaxed again. "Only, he spends most of his time offshore on the rigs, and there's me, all alone, with my dreams of the Beast, in our pretty little house with its pretty little garden. And I decided, what the place really needs is a Beast of its own."

A pause. Izzie stared earnestly around the room.

"Get on with it," called a voice from the back. Stu Cosby. Zoe realised what being a 'traditionalist' meant.

"Nearly done," replied Izzie, smiling, as the crowd shushed Cosby. "What I did, then, is I found myself an ironsmith. Old Jimmy Metal, he calls himself, although I'm not asking you to believe that's his real name. All I know is, he's an artist. What that man can do with his hands..."

She shivered theatrically, and continued. "And he's skilled professionally, too," she said with a wink. "He's built me a twenty-foot model of the Beast in steel and iron and put it up in my back garden. And yes, I've spent every penny me and the husband saved for more than a decade, but I promise you it was worth it."

"Come on," called Cosby. "There's a time limit!"

Izzie ignored him. "And the thing is," she said, "Nat's due back from the rigs any day now, so what's a girl to do?"

She surveyed the crowd. Zoe followed her gaze, and was surprised to see that the woman she'd spotted earlier was still scowling at the stage, her face twisted in what looked a lot like hatred. Maybe Stu Cosby wasn't the only 'traditionalist' in the room.

"I'll tell you what I've done, anyway. I've shacked up with Old Jimmy and changed the locks, and when Nat makes it back from the North Sea, he'll be in for the shock of his life." Izzie ended, bowed at the audience, and exited the stage through a small door in the rear.

The crowd went wild. The story itself had been decent enough. But even a newcomer like Zoe could tell the delivery was something special.

Izzie would have been a tough act for even a decent competitor to follow, but the next liar on stage wasn't close to decent. Sid Carmichael spoke so quietly Zoe struggled to make out most of the words, and the bits she did hear seemed to be a confused ramble about aerial dogfights during the Second World War.

There was a short break while Sid left the stage to a smattering of polite applause. The screen was finally working, the words 'WORLD'S BIGGEST LIAR' marked out in black on a white background.

The next competitor was an earnest-looking twentysomething called Alan, who bounded onto the stage with the energy of youth, grabbed the microphone, and shouted something incomprehensible.

"What's that?" called the white-haired man who'd spoken to Carl earlier.

"There's a dead woman in the dressing room!" shouted Alan.

"Very good," the white-haired man shouted back.

"I mean it," said Alan.

There was laughter in the crowd, and a little applause. Alan's eyes were wide, and what Zoe had thought of as the energy of youth now looked more like an excellent impression of a man in the throes of panic.

"Love it," shouted someone from behind. "Hanging from the ceiling, is she?"

The crowd laughed its approval.

"No, really," Alan insisted. "There's a dead woman. She's... It's horrible."

He was an excellent actor. The eyes. The way he stood there, stock still, then moved, then stopped again.

"I'm not joking," Alan shouted. "Is there a police officer in the room?"

The young man had nailed the part. It was so authentic, it could almost be...

Zoe turned to Carl and saw her own thoughts reflected in his eyes. Without a word, the two of them stood.

"Are you police officers?" Alan shouted, spotting them.

"Yes," Zoe called back.

"Sit down," shouted someone from behind, but Zoe ignored it.

"Come on," Alan said, heading for the door at the back. Zoe and Carl followed him onto the stage, through the door, and into a short, dark corridor with another door set in one wall. Alan went to turn the handle, but Zoe pushed him out of the way, wrapped her hand in the napkin she'd grabbed from the table, and turned it herself.

The dressing room was a small space. A mirror, a little desk, three chairs.

On the middle chair, right in front of the mirror, sat Izzie Hopkirk. She was pale and unmoving. As Zoe reached for her neck to check her pulse, she saw dark marks there. Bruises that hadn't been present when Izzie had been on stage just minutes earlier.

Zoe waited, counted, waited. Nothing. No pulse.

Izzie Hopkirk was dead.

CHAPTER TWO

"Gloves," Zoe said.

"What?" asked Carl.

She turned from the corpse to him, briefly irritated, then remembered.

This wasn't work. Carl wasn't one of her team. He didn't know the way she worked.

"My bag," she said. "In the—"

"On it." He left the room.

It wasn't like they hadn't worked together before. They'd even interviewed suspects together. But this was the raw edge of what she did, the point where instincts merged with years of familiar processes and things just flowed. A side of her Carl had never seen.

He was back a moment later, bag open, handing her the gloves.

"Another pair for yourself," she said. The young man was still there – Alan, wasn't it?

She turned to say something, but Carl was already gloved

and pushing the man gently out of the room, telling him to wait but not to come back in until he was called for.

"How the hell did this happen?" he asked.

Zoe had already grabbed her phone. "Dr Robertson will confirm, but it looks like she's been strangled."

Carl frowned at her. That wasn't what he'd meant.

"Who do you need?" he asked.

She paused and looked around the room. Forensics first. Izzie Hopkirk had been dead a matter of minutes, and whoever had killed her would surely have left some trace of themself behind.

"Stella," she said. "Then the team. Then Chris."

"I'll call Chris," he said.

She smiled in gratitude. Chris Robertson was the area pathologist. If there was anything to be learned from Izzie Hopkirk's body, he'd find that, too.

Stella answered with her customary joyfulness.

"Fuck's sake," she said. "I thought you were on a day off."

"People die even when I'm on leave," Zoe replied, and explained where she was and what had happened.

"Santon Bridge?" Stella replied. "I can be with you in thirty minutes." As Zoe ended the call, Carl turned to her, his own phone pressed to his ear, and mouthed the words 'half an hour', which made sense. Chris Robertson would probably be somewhere underground in the mortuary section of the hospital right next to the enterprise park that housed Stella's team. She wondered which of them would get there first.

Zoe hesitated before making her next call. Normally she'd have spoken to Aaron, but he was still on his month off, coming to terms with his own near-death experience. On the mend, he'd told her. But probably not ready for another dead body.

Nina answered on the first ring, much like Stella, but without the swearing.

"Boss? Thought you were on a day off."

"We were," Zoe replied. "Are. I'm at the Bridge Inn with DI Whaley. A woman's been murdered."

"Bloody hell."

"Bloody hell indeed. See you soon?"

"Twenty-five minutes," Nina replied. The Hub was no closer than the hospital or the enterprise park, but Nina was Nina.

She turned to the doorway at the sound of voices from the corridor. Whatever Alan had said, it hadn't calmed things down. Carl was standing in the doorway, blocking the view of anyone who came too close.

They could shut the door. But the small room was hot. Airless. And shutting the door would be just one more disturbance to a crime scene that had already been disturbed more than it should have.

"Forensic suit," she said, and Carl nodded. He knew she kept them in the car. She ducked under his arm and found herself faced with the beginning of what looked worryingly like a mob. She glanced back, and was reassured. They wouldn't mess with Carl.

"Don't come any closer," she said, and started to push her way through.

CHAPTER THREE

"OK, everyone, can you please stand back?" Carl said.

No one moved. There were ten, maybe fifteen of them in the short corridor between the stage and the dressing room. Behind them, the door to the stage was open, and a steady hum of murmuring voices filtered through.

"I need to keep this area clear," he said.

"Thought you weren't taking part," said a voice. Carl peered through the crowd. It was the white-haired man they'd been sitting by during the performance.

"I'm sorry?" he said.

"I asked if you were taking part and you said no. Looks like you were having me on, young man."

For Christ's sake.

"Look," Carl said, trying to project a sense of calm. "I'm Detective Inspector Carl Whaley. Cumbria Police."

No need to mention PSD. They wouldn't understand even if he did.

"Let's see your badge, then," demanded a rabbit-toothed woman near the front.

CHAPTER THREE

"Warrant card," muttered Carl, as he pulled it out and flipped it open.

"Ooh, look at that," said the woman. She reached for it, and he pulled it back. "How do I know it's real?"

"Real?" he repeated.

The woman had turned away to address the rest of the crowd.

"It looks real," she said, "but it might not be. For all I know, he could have just bought it off t' internet."

There were rumbles of agreement. Where the hell was the manager? He'd asked that young man, Alan, to find someone and bring them here.

"Listen," he began. They were edging towards him. "Listen," he said, much louder, and the movement stopped. "There's been a serious incident and I need you all to leave the area."

"It's very convincing," said a voice from somewhere in the crowd.

"Told me he wasn't taking part," said the white-haired man, sounding positively aggrieved that he'd been misled. Ridiculous, given the event he'd turned up to was the World's Biggest Liar competition.

And, Carl reminded himself, he wasn't misleading anyone.

"What's in the room?" said the woman who'd wanted his warrant card.

"As I say," Carl replied, "there's been a serious incident, and I—"

"Out the way!" called another voice. "Let dog see rabbit!"

"A serious incident," Carl repeated, "and I need to preserve the scene."

"Ooh, what's this?" asked someone, and Carl sensed

movement in the crowd, individuals pushing themselves to the side to make room for someone coming through. He tensed, and moved his feet a little further apart for stability.

It was Zoe. In her forensic suit.

"Is this part of it?" said someone.

"It's very convincing," said the person who'd made the same comment earlier.

"Are you allowed costumes?" complained a voice. "And two of them working together, is that really in the—"

Zoe had reached the front now. Carl stepped briefly aside, and before she disappeared behind him, she gave him a wink.

"Stop it!" he shouted, and to his surprise, they fell silent.

"This is not an act. We are not in the World's Biggest Liar competition. We are police officers. A woman has lost her life, and you need to do as we ask."

He stopped. They were edging away from him now, as if they'd just learned he had a contagious disease.

"You only had to ask," said the rabbit-toothed woman, looking genuinely upset now. "If you'd said all that at the start, we might have listened."

Carl simply smiled and thanked her for her cooperation. Sometimes, there was no point in arguing. And he had work to do.

He edged his way past them all, into the main bar. Whoever had done this could well have left before they'd found Izzie's body. But if they hadn't, he didn't want them leaving now.

CHAPTER FOUR

"Will you stop complaining?"

DC Nina Kapoor parked outside the Bridge Inn, and DC Tom Willis emerged from her car with the look of someone who'd just been released from death row.

"I didn't say anything!" he insisted.

"You didn't have to," she replied. "I saw your face. And you were brushing yourself down. I've just cleaned up in there."

She glared at him. He gave her a sheepish smile, then reached forward and pulled something out of her hair. She grimaced.

He held it up. A single McDonald's fry.

"It was on the headrest," he told her. "I think there's more."

"Fine." Nina turned and walked towards the pub, and Tom followed.

There were two patrol cars there already. Inside, she could see Harriett Barnes and Roddy Chen. It was good to have Roddy back, and he and Harriett worked well as a team. Tom seemed to be over Harriett, too, finally.

They walked through the bar to the main function room, where the bulk of the crowd seemed to be assembled. Nina could hear Tom muttering beside her.

"Chaos," he was saying.

There were people there who didn't seem to know what had happened, frowning in confusion and asking what was going on. There were people who knew *something* had happened, but assumed it was part of the entertainment. A handful were actually applauding Harriett and Roddy, and one woman had her hands on Roddy's uniform, feeling it, exclaiming at how impressive it was.

"Must have spent a fortune on the outfits," she said.

And then there was the third group. Those who knew what had happened, and knew it was real. They whispered amongst themselves, and it spread like a ripple through the crowd. The excitement dying down. The confusion replaced by horror.

DI Finch was standing at the front. She picked up a microphone.

"Hello, everyone," she said. The muttering stopped. "I'm DI Zoe Finch, from West Cumbria CID. As you may have heard, there's been a serious incident here at the pub, and unfortunately, a woman has lost her life. No, this isn't a joke, or a lie, or anything to do with the entertainment here. It's real, and we need to investigate it. OK?"

The boss surveyed the room. Nobody spoke.

"Good," she continued. "We need your cooperation, so I'd like you all to stay here until my colleagues have spoken to you, taken details, and told you that you can leave." She pointed to Nina and Tom, and to Roddy and Harriett. Nina

CHAPTER FOUR

saw heads swivel briefly in her direction before returning to the boss.

"In the meantime, I'd be grateful if you could try not to talk among yourselves. And don't go phoning people or putting stories up on social media. A woman has died and we need to get to the bottom of it. OK?"

Another silence.

"Good. Please be patient. I can assure you, we'll get to you as soon as possible. Thank you."

She put the mic back on its stand and beckoned to Nina and Tom, who went up to the stage to join her.

"Can you take statements?" she asked.

They both nodded.

"Good. Everyone here. The other competitors in particular, they all had access to the dressing room. Oh, and make sure you get one from Stu Cosby."

"Who?" asked Nina.

"He's a regular," said Tom. "I've seen him on YouTube. Why him?"

"The woman who died was another competitor," explained the DI. "Stu Cosby didn't seem to like her very much. Do you think Harriett and Roddy can handle the crowd? Carl can help them."

Nina looked around the room. DI Whaley was running crowd control with the PCs. There was the odd whispered conversation, but it was next to impossible to do anything about that, not with so many people in a confined space. And if they were allowed to wait outside, no doubt some of them would take the opportunity to slip away.

It was as good as it was going to get.

Ten minutes later, Nina was sitting at a table by the bar talking to a nervous-looking young man named Alan Miller, who was explaining how he'd found the body and how nobody had believed him for so long, he'd started to doubt himself.

"Horrible," he said. "It was horrible. It was... She really is dead, isn't she?"

Nina nodded. "I'm sorry, Mr Miller. Did you know her?"

"No," he replied. "But I heard her, doing her thing. She was very good. I just can't believe it."

Nina was running through the details for the second time, making sure she hadn't missed anything, when she noticed movement in the function room.

"Wait here," she told Alan.

A man was pushing his way through the crowd, past DI Whaley and towards the bar, stopping only when he found himself blocked by the enormous figure of Roddy Chen.

"Is it her?" he said.

Nina approached the man. "What do you mean?" she asked, from behind Roddy's shoulder.

"Is it Izzie? Izzie Hopkirk? That's what someone said, and I can't... It can't be her, can it?"

"I'm sorry, Mr...?"

He stared at her for a moment, then nodded. "Hopkirk. Nathan Hopkirk. Izzie's my wife."

CHAPTER FIVE

Zoe left Stella and Dr Robertson working quietly in the dressing room, Caroline Deane standing outside and passing items to Stella as she demanded them.

She followed Nina past the stage, through the function room, where Carl shrugged helplessly at her, to the bar area, where a man leaned with one elbow on the bar, his eyes wet, his mouth open in what looked like disbelief.

There was something familiar about his narrow eyes, his carefully shaved stubble and short, neatly groomed hair.

"Is it her?" he asked, as Zoe approached him.

"I'm sorry, Mr Hopkirk," she said.

The tears came a moment later, his breathing ragged as his body shook. The barmaid caught Zoe's eye and pointed to a row of spirits. Zoe nodded, and a moment later Nathan Hopkirk had a whisky in one hand while he rubbed at his eyes with the other.

"I don't understand," he said as Zoe led him to a table. "She was... I saw her. I saw her on stage. And then... I just don't get it."

The story came out slowly. Nathan had only returned from the North Sea that day, back from the rigs for three weeks. Izzie had told him to meet her at the Bridge Inn, and he'd turned up, in his hired car, having got lost on the way. He'd been born and raised in Whitehaven – as had Izzie – but he'd never come across this Santon Bridge before.

"I came in, and there she was, on stage. I didn't know what to think. It was supposed to be a surprise, I suppose. She hadn't told me."

Zoe looked closely at him. "You turned up during her act, right?"

Nathan nodded. He'd been the one who'd pushed into the room, past Stu Cosby.

"Tell me about Izzie," she said.

Nathan took a sip of his whisky. "Well, we're both forty, her and me. Been married..." He frowned. "Fourteen years in April. She works in forestry products."

"What's that?" Zoe asked.

"Timber," he explained. "She's in the office."

Timber, then. Port of Workington. Zoe sighed. *Myron Carter's kingdom.*

But surely this didn't involve Myron Carter. Not everything had to involve Myron Carter.

Meanwhile, Nathan Hopkirk was still talking about his wife in the present tense.

"And you, Mr Hopkirk?" Zoe asked. "You're on the rigs, then?"

"That's right." He nodded. "North Sea. I'm out there months at a time, but good long breaks."

"No kids?"

"Neither of us wants kids. Wanted kids." His face began to crumple before he gave a sharp little nod, gritted his teeth,

CHAPTER FIVE

and continued. "The plan was early retirement. Travel the world. Enjoy ourselves."

The tears came again, and no amount of sharp little nods could hold them back. Zoe waited as he controlled himself, gulping down the whisky. Behind the bar, another was already poured.

Zoe looked around the room, and through the doorway into the function room. Tom and Nina were getting through the witnesses, but there were a lot of them. They'd be here a while.

A woman was standing near Roddy, eyeing the gap between him and the door. She looked like she was thinking of making a break for it.

Zoe had seen that woman before. In her fifties, thick glasses, hair piled messily on top of her head – she'd been the one scowling as Izzie told her tales.

"Can you wait here just one moment," she said, and Nathan Hopkirk nodded.

At the other end of the bar, Tom was making notes as a woman stood up to leave. Zoe walked over and sat down before he could start speaking to anyone else.

"The woman there," she said, pointing back at the door, noting the woman scowl again as she spotted them looking in her direction. "She was here when Izzie was speaking."

"They all were," Tom pointed out. "Most of them thought she was brilliant."

"But this one didn't. She looked furious. Speak to her next, OK?"

CHAPTER SIX

"Marion Baker," Tom said.

"Mrs Baker," the woman corrected.

"First name Marion?"

"Yes, that's true."

Mrs Baker wore a plain grey cardigan with a white blouse, and a pair of black trousers that looked like they could do with a press. She hadn't been pleased to be summoned, and nothing Tom had said since then seemed to have improved her mood.

He tried offering her a drink from the bar, and she gave a theatrical little sniff of disgust.

"I'm driving," she told him. "And I don't think you should be encouraging me to drink."

"Perhaps a soft drink?" he suggested. "Or a cup of tea?"

"I'd rather get all this over and done with, if you don't mind."

"Did you know Izzie Hopkirk?" he asked.

She sat back and watched him in silence for a moment before she answered.

CHAPTER SIX

"So it is her," she said.

"It is."

"Well, yes, then. I knew her. Used to work with her. And I can't say I'm surprised."

Tom blinked. "You're not surprised by what, Mrs Baker?"

"I'm not surprised she finally made someone angry enough to kill her."

Tom had to fight to stop his own surprise from showing. People tended not to speak that way about the recently murdered. Even if they absolutely hated them.

"Why's that?" he asked, his gaze drawn past her to Harriett Barnes, who was walking through the crowd alongside Caroline Deane, the two of them cradling an evidence bag each in their arms.

He was over Harriett now. He was sure of it. And all that nonsense the boss had said, about her being PSD. It was possible, he supposed. But it wasn't exactly likely.

"She wasn't a nice person, Constable," Marion replied. "Selfish, I'd say."

She looked past him and grunted a greeting at someone else. Tom turned.

The husband. Nathan Hopkirk. He was looking past the boss and nodding back at Marion Barker.

It wasn't friendly, on either side. But it wasn't hostile, either.

CHAPTER SEVEN

Zoe had spoken to a lot of bereaved people over the years, but it wasn't the sort of thing you became immune to. And Nathan Hopkirk was one of the more obvious cases.

He was trying to hide it. But he was heartbroken. Painfully and completely heartbroken.

She'd finished taking his initial statement, and asked him to wait, not that he really had much choice. She'd just watched him knock back three neat whiskies and there was another sitting in front of him. He wouldn't be driving that hire car any time soon.

She heard her name, and turned to see Stella and Chris Robertson approaching through the function room. She nodded to a quiet corner of the bar, and joined them there, the three of them standing around a tall table and speaking quietly.

"Anything?" she asked Chris.

"With the usual provisos about what I might find in the post-mortem, looks like she's been strangled. I gather you don't need a time of death, but I can tell you it was recent."

"I saw her onstage about an hour ago, so it was definitely recent."

Chris nodded. "No obvious sign of any defensive wounds. In fact, apart from the bruising on her neck, she looks like she was in excellent shape."

"That, and the fact that she's dead," Stella observed.

Stella seemed to be in an even sourer mood than usual, and Zoe thought she knew why. Chris excused himself to attend to the body, and Zoe turned to the crime scene manager.

"Everything OK, Stella?" she asked.

"Again, apart from the dead woman, yes."

"Nothing to do with Carl being here, then?"

Stella glared at her, then shrugged.

"I know it wasn't his fault," she said. "I just can't stop thinking how it might have been different."

It, in this case, was what had happened to Hussein Mahmoud. Huz. One of Stella's team, until he'd been pulled in by PSD, questioned, and admitted to his role in a drugs operation.

And then he'd been released, and murdered, and everyone seemed to be blaming themselves for it. Zoe had lain awake nights, wondering if she'd done something wrong. Aaron was sure it was all his fault. Everyone blamed themselves. Except for Stella, who blamed PSD.

"Look, Stella," Zoe began.

"No. Look, I'm sorry. I know it's stupid. Fucking hell, I'm the one who sent him packing before that bastard killed him. Forget it. I just..."

"Stella—"

"I said, forget it," Stella said, in a tone that brooked no disagreement. "Now, your current body, there's nothing obvious, like the doc said, but the killer's probably left DNA on it somewhere."

"Even if they've got gloves on?"

Stella nodded. "We've taken out some of the furniture for analysis. Things people might have bumped against. Left some clothing attached to it, maybe. Even if she got taken by surprise, she might have made the killer work. Anything can happen."

"Good. Show me." Zoe followed Stella through the function room and along the corridor back to the dressing room.

The place was covered in plastic sheeting, with protective covers over the floor and the more significant objects that hadn't yet been removed: a chair, a door handle, the desk, the mirror. Caroline Deane was bent over in the corner, pulling something up from the floor with a pair of tweezers. Chris Robertson was directing his 'lad', the two of them examining the body and working out the best way of removing it from the scene and back to the mortuary.

There was nothing for Zoe in here. She'd find Carl, speak to some more witnesses.

There were dozens of them. And the place wasn't big.

Someone had to have seen something.

CHAPTER EIGHT

"Look, I'm sorry she's dead, of course I am, I wouldn't wish that on anyone, but really, you can't expect everyone here to turn their lives upside-down for her."

Stu Cosby looked at Nina as he spoke, his eyebrows raised in expectation. Then he fell silent.

What was he hoping for? A round of applause?

"Take me back please, Mr Cosby," Nina said.

"With pleasure." Cosby smiled.

As far as he was concerned, this was all an unfortunate inconvenience. Once he was home, he'd probably forget he'd ever come across Izzie Hopkirk. Given the alcohol Nina could smell on his breath, he might forget even sooner.

"Had you ever met Izzie before today?"

"I think I'd have remembered her, don't you?" he replied.

"I didn't have the opportunity to meet her before she died, Mr Cosby. Tell me about your impressions of her, if you don't mind."

Cosby leaned across the table and spoke confidentially.

"Look," he said, "I think we all know why she wasn't very popular, don't we?"

"Do we?" Nina asked.

Everyone else she'd spoken to seemed to have been taken with Izzie Hopkirk. They hadn't known her personally. But up there on the stage, she'd made quite the impression.

"We do, DC Kapoor. We do. She wasn't really part of the community, you see."

Nina felt her throat tighten. "The community?"

"Indeed." Cosby nodded, an earnest expression on his face. "It really wasn't her place to be here, and I think we all realised that rather quickly."

He made a sweeping gesture, as if to take in all the people who had supposedly realised it wasn't Izzie Hopkirk's place to be at the Bridge Inn performing at the World's Biggest Liar competition.

"She was from Whitehaven, Mr Cosby," Nina pointed out. "Born there, lived there all her life. If that doesn't make her part of the community, then what exactly does?"

Nina knew the answer. She'd come across it herself, often enough. She was surprised it had happened to a white woman, but, on reflection, only a little surprised. There were clubs where even being white wasn't enough.

"City folk," sniffed Cosby.

Nina eyed him. *City folk, my arse. Women, more like.* She was about to voice this when a commotion close by drew her attention.

Nathan Hopkirk was on his feet. He rose clumsily and pushed his way through to the function room, past Roddy, elbowing people out of the way as he went.

Nina stood. "Mr Hopkirk!" she shouted.

He turned. "I need to see her," he called back, and continued to push through.

Nina followed in his wake, past bemused onlookers. The boss's partner, DI Whaley, was in front of her, just a few steps behind Nathan Hopkirk, but the widower was already past the stage and through the door leading to the corridor.

"Shit," said Nina, and started to run. DI Whaley was doing the same thing, but a second too late.

By the time Nina reached the dressing room, Nathan Hopkirk was inside. Caroline was still crouched in the corner, looking on in astonishment. Dr Robertson was nowhere to be seen, but his intern, a tall, willowy young man who seemed years too young for the role, was staring in horror at the scene in the middle of the room.

Nathan Hopkirk had grabbed his wife's corpse and lifted it from the chair. He was hugging it tight, the dead woman's head pressed into his shoulder as he shook, and wept, and said her name over and over again.

CHAPTER NINE

One thing, Carl had been asked to do. Help the uniforms. Keep order.

One thing.

"Mr Hopkirk," he said, quieter than the last time.

The man turned to him, tears in his eyes. Carl reached for his arm, and Hopkirk allowed Carl to lead him gently up and out of the room, through the corridor to the function room, past a hundred curious eyes, and into the bar.

"I'm sorry," said Hopkirk. He'd been muttering his wife's name, in the dressing room, repeating it again and again, but now all he seemed capable of doing was apologising. Carl kept telling him it was OK, but he didn't want to stop.

"Have a drink," Carl suggested, and Hopkirk nodded slowly, sadly. There had been a lot of drinks. Carl wasn't sure who'd end up paying for them. But one more wouldn't hurt.

It wasn't one more, though. It was four. Four more whiskies while Carl sat and spoke with Nathan Hopkirk, letting the man apologise, and say his wife's name, listening while he recalled the places they'd been and the things they'd done, while he listed the places they'd planned to go and the things they hoped to do.

It was tragic. It was awful. And Nathan Hopkirk was drunk.

"Mr Hopkirk," Carl said, finally. "I think you should go home now. I know DI Finch and her team will want to speak to you again, but I'm not sure now's a good time. Is there anyone here who can drive you home? Any friends?"

Hopkirk shook his head.

"Is there anyone you'd like me to call, Mr Hopkirk?"

"Nat," said Nathan Hopkirk. "I wish people would stop calling me 'Mr Hopkirk.' It's Nat. Just Nat."

"Nat. Is there anyone you'd like to call? Maybe someone who can take you home? Or someone you can stay with?"

Nat shook his head. "I just want to go home. By myself."

Carl looked around the room until he spotted Zoe talking to Sid Carmichael, the competitor who'd had the bad luck of following Izzie Hopkirk onto the stage.

Still, better that than dead.

"Wait here a moment," Carl said, and asked Nat for his car keys. The man handed them over without a word.

Carl didn't like the idea of him going back to an empty house alone. He told Zoe what he was planning and a few minutes later, he was propping Nat up in the car park.

"Your car," he said, "What is it?"

Nat frowned, then pointed at a BMW at the far end of the still-crowded car park.

"Hired it for a few weeks," he sniffed. "No point owning one when I'm on the rigs. And Izzie has one..." He drew in a breath. "Had."

CHAPTER TEN

Zoe watched as Izzie Hopkirk's body was manoeuvred out of the dressing room by Chris Robertson and his intern.

"This is Dave," said Chris, as he wheeled the front end past her.

"Xavier," muttered the intern as he followed behind.

Someone from the Bridge Inn had produced a key and opened a door Zoe hadn't even noticed, set into the end of the corridor. It opened onto a small yard into which an ambulance had been squeezed with the same sort of skill and attention Chris and Xavier were paying to the corpse. Thank God they didn't have to wheel the late Izzie Hopkirk past the remaining twenty or so witnesses in the function room and the bar area.

As she turned to head back into the function room, her phone rang.

Not now.

After eleven rings, it stopped, and she emerged from the corridor onto the stage.

Her phone started ringing again. Shaking her head, she

CHAPTER TEN

pulled off one glove and checked the display. Her frown turned to a smile.

"Aaron," she said, her phone against her shoulder as she pulled off the other glove. "I'd say it's great to hear from you, but your timing's terrible."

"Why?" he asked. "Is something wrong?"

She listened for signs of panic in his voice. But he just sounded like an ordinary person asking an ordinary question.

"Just another murder, Aaron. Nothing you need worry about."

"Is it..."

Zoe turned away from the room and headed back to the corridor. "What?"

"Is it something to do with Carter?"

She frowned. But he wasn't in a flat spin. He was just asking.

"Don't think so. Not sure yet. All a bit odd, really. But most importantly, Aaron, it's not your problem."

He laughed, the best thing she'd heard all day.

"Actually, it might be, soon. I was hoping I could come back. Doc says it's OK."

"Limited duties?" she asked.

"Of course. Obviously, I don't think that's necessary, but that's what the rules say, and Dr Filey insists, so I haven't really got a leg to stand on, have I?"

She smiled. "No, Aaron, you haven't. OK, listen. I'll have a word with the super. It's her call, ultimately, and this has been quicker than we expected."

"Which is good news, isn't it, boss?"

Now she was the one laughing.

"Excellent news, Aaron. Just bear with me. I'll speak to you in the morning."

She ended the call and caught Nina's eye just as the DC was finishing up with one of the bar staff. Together, they waited for Tom to finish interviewing one of the spectators, the white-haired man, who walked away shaking his head and muttering, "I really didn't believe it. I really didn't."

"What have you got?" Zoe asked.

Tom looked at Nina, who shrugged. "Not a lot, boss. Most of them know nothing. No, scratch that. They all know nothing. Most of them know nothing and are horrified by the murder."

"Most?"

"Stu Cosby, boss. The—"

"I know who he is, Nina. What did he have to say?"

"Doesn't think Izzie was *part of the community*, as he put it."

"Didn't like a woman crashing his party, more like," Zoe replied.

Nina nodded. "That's the impression I got. Not that it's a motive for murder, but he's the only one who had a bad word to say."

Zoe nodded and turned to Tom.

"Much the same, boss, only my version of Stu Cosby is Marion Baker."

"Who?"

"The woman you pointed out to me. The one with the glasses and..." He mimed a mass of hair being coiled around the top of his head.

Zoe raised an eyebrow. "OK, what about her?"

"She didn't like Izzie at all. Said she wasn't surprised Izzie finally made someone angry enough to kill her."

"The milk of human kindness turned sour with that one," observed Nina.

CHAPTER TEN

"Right," continued Tom. "She said she used to work with Izzie. Called her 'selfish'. Obviously, she insisted she didn't know anything about the murder. And I could be wrong, but I think she knew the husband, Nathan. They sort of grunted at each other."

"Like enemies?" Zoe asked.

"Not like enemies, no. But not like friends, either."

"Like people who'd come across each other because one of them worked with the other's wife?"

"I suppose so," said Tom. "But it's like Nina's lot, really. Nothing out of the ordinary from anyone except that one person."

Zoe nodded. "OK. Let's get through the last few and leave it for now. Tomorrow, I'll want to speak to the husband again, as well as Baker and Cosby."

Baker and Cosby. It sounded like a comedy show. Maybe they'd have something worth listening to tomorrow.

CHAPTER ELEVEN

IN THE PASSENGER seat of the BMW, Nat Hopkirk shook his head and stared out at the hills and the houses.

"Is there anyone you want me to call?" Carl asked. The man was a wreck. Carl couldn't blame him. He was grieving, and drunk, and on his way back to an empty house he hadn't seen in months.

Silence. Carl looked across, and Nat shook his head.

"Just leave it, yeah? Just drop me home, Mr... No. DI, isn't it? DI Whalley?"

"Whaley," corrected Carl. "If you're sure..."

Hopkirk said nothing, and the journey continued in silence. The house was in Mirehouse, at the south end of Whitehaven. Hopkirk pointed out a neat semi on Derwentwater Road that was more impressive than the building Izzie had described in her monologue.

But that had all been a lie, of course. So much had happened since then, Carl had almost forgotten why they'd been at the Bridge Inn in the first place.

CHAPTER ELEVEN

"This'll do," said Hopkirk. He had the door open before Carl had brought the car to a halt.

"I'll just come in with you, check..."

Check what, exactly? Nat Hopkirk didn't want him there. But Carl couldn't just walk away.

"Suit yourself," Hopkirk replied.

Carl's phone pinged as he parked and opened the door.

A text from the estate agent. They'd had their eye on a house in the centre of town. A fun place. A hot tub in the garden. It was more *them* than the place they were in at the moment. More Zoe, really, but Carl liked it, too.

'Dear Mr and Mrs Whaley,' it began, and Carl resisted the urge to chuckle. *Mrs Whaley*. Zoe wouldn't like that. He looked up to see Hopkirk standing by what looked like a gate to the back garden, peering over, his small suitcase in one hand. Months away, one small suitcase. The man travelled light.

"Are you OK?" Carl called, and winced.

His wife had just been murdered. Of course he wasn't OK.

Hopkirk turned slowly back to him, and walked even more slowly to the back door. Carl glanced down and scanned the rest of a long and highly formal text, skipping over sentences and picking out the important words.

Pleased to inform you...

That was promising.

Hopkirk was at the front door now, struggling with his keys. Carl walked over to him, eyes darting between his phone, the path, and the widower.

Our clients have accepted your offer.

Yes.

Carl felt an urge to shout it out.

Zoe. He had to call Zoe. But he couldn't.

He stood by Hopkirk and watched as he fiddled with the keys, putting the wrong one in three times before he got it right.

"I don't spend much time here," Hopkirk said, as the key finally turned. Both men sighed in relief, and Hopkirk burst into tears. Carl touched his arm, and waited for it to subside.

"Sorry," said Hopkirk.

"You don't need to apologise."

Hopkirk shrugged and pushed the door open. Carl glanced down again.

Pending appointment of solicitors...

Inside, the house didn't have the feel of somewhere that had been empty for long – but it hadn't, had it? Izzie had only left the place this morning. Left this morning, expecting to be back this afternoon with her husband.

Life could move fast. But death could give it a run for its money.

Inside, Hopkirk switched on a light. Carl followed him through a kitchen to a wood-floored living room with a big TV and a leather sofa and armchair.

"Do you want me to stay?" asked Carl, checking his phone again.

Please indicate your acceptance of...

Hopkirk had already opened a wooden cabinet in the corner of the room and extracted a bottle of whisky and a glass. A single glass.

"Would you like me to—" Carl began.

Hopkirk shook his head. "Look," he said, "I know you think you've got to keep me company, and I know what this looks like." He gestured at the bottle. "But what do you expect? I'm not gonna kill myself, if that's what you're worrying about."

"It's just..."

What could he do? Watch the man while he drank himself to sleep?

"I really don't mind sticking around," Carl offered, but Hopkirk shook his head again.

"Look, don't take this the wrong way, DI Whalley, but we're not friends. I'm sure you're a great guy and everything, but right now I just want to sit down by myself and drink whisky until I pass out. Can you let me do that?"

Carl nodded. He'd probably have wanted to do the same thing himself.

CHAPTER TWELVE

Zoe raised her bottle of zero-alcohol beer and clinked it against Carl's lager. She shook her head, grinning. Carl hadn't been able to keep the smile off his face, and she wasn't far behind him.

It had been a difficult day with a tragic event at the heart of it, but that house...

It was almost everything she wanted. Other than the fact that it was in Cumbria, which she was still warming to, it really was everything she wanted.

And while Carl was in a good mood, she thought she'd take advantage of it.

"Don't you think we've got enough now?"

"Enough?"

He was watching her through narrowed eyes. He knew exactly what she meant. But she spelled it out anyway.

"To bring in Streeting."

They'd been through this disagreement a dozen times. But she still couldn't persuade Carl to see it her way.

And he was probably right.

CHAPTER TWELVE

In her efforts to get something that would stick on Myron Carter, the local organised crime boss, Zoe had kept in contact with Olivia Bagsby, an artist who'd captured some potentially valuable evidence on film. Olivia had been on the run ever since, suspecting that if Cumbria CID found out where she was, Carter wouldn't be far behind.

But a few weeks earlier, Olivia had finally sent Zoe her photos, and what they showed was almost good enough to be considered evidence. Almost.

Zoe sighed. "Do you think he'll be OK?" she asked.

"Who?"

"Nat Hopkirk."

A shrug, followed by a frown. "Who knows? I wouldn't be. I don't think he'll kill himself. He assured me of that. He wants to drink himself to sleep, and honestly, I don't blame him."

"Everything else OK?" Zoe asked.

He took a long swig from his bottle and shook his head.

"I don't know," he said. "There's something from today... I've seen something, and it doesn't quite add up. But I can't think what it is."

"Is it possible," Zoe asked, "that it's simply the effect of an unexpected murder, followed by three bottles of premium strength lager drunk in the space of twenty-five minutes?"

She pointed to the two empties and the almost-finished bottle.

Carl grinned. "Maybe it is," he said. "Here's to the house."

"Here's to the house," she replied, and drank.

CHAPTER THIRTEEN

"Just can't keep away from murder, can you?"

Fiona was smiling at her, which was a relief, as you could never be sure when the super was serious.

"Believe me," Zoe said, "all I wanted was a nice normal day off."

"You should have stayed in Birmingham if you'd wanted something like that," countered Fiona.

Zoe swallowed, suddenly seeing her favourite places, the parks and restaurants, even New Street Station and the bloody red cage car park. Fiona was only joking, but the words exposed something.

Cumbria was beautiful. Whitehaven was interesting, and the house, if they got it, would be fun.

But would it ever be home?

"Tell me you've got a suspect, at least," Fiona continued.

Zoe offered a grimace. "I wish. And yes, I know. We were there. Two DIs, a murder committed a few feet away, and we didn't see a thing."

"Forensics?"

CHAPTER THIRTEEN

"They've pulled all manner of prints and things. But there were lots of people going in and out. It's not going to be easy. We're struggling for motive, too. There's a couple of people who clearly didn't like the victim, and we're bringing them in this morning, but it seems a bit of a stretch for either of them to have killed her."

"You know as well as I do that murder always seems implausible until it happens."

Zoe nodded. People killed over all manner of things, the big things, and the ones so small you could barely see them.

"But look, Zoe, all joking aside, you're going to have to find this person."

Zoe blinked. *Find this person?* That was her job, wasn't it? Of course she'd find them.

"Of course I will, Fiona," she said.

"Oh, I know. Because if you don't... Well, it would be a little humiliating, wouldn't it?"

"I'm sorry?"

"As you just said yourself, Zoe. Star of Cumbria CID and her PSD partner sitting there while someone commits a murder. It wouldn't play well in the press."

"I was joking," Zoe pointed out.

But Fiona gave her a half-smile that had no mirth in it at all. "I wasn't. Was there something else you wanted to talk to me about?"

Zoe took a breath. "I had a call from Aaron Keyes yesterday. He's been signed off by Dr Filey. He's ready to come back."

"Limited duties?"

"Of course."

"And what do you think, Zoe?"

"I'm keen to bring him back in as soon as possible."

"Hmmm." Fiona frowned, picked up a pen from her desk, and passed it through her fingers. "It's difficult, this sort of thing. All sorts of potential blowback."

"Really?" Zoe had assumed Fiona would be delighted. "Like what?"

"If anything goes wrong. If he makes a mistake."

"He's a DS in my team, Fiona. He'll be on limited duties until we're sure he's ready for more. He's not a firearms officer. He's good at his job and he can prove that without taking any risks."

"And you're sure of that, are you?"

"Yes," Zoe replied with a frown.

"You took longer to answer that than makes me comfortable, Zoe."

"I just... I haven't actually seen him in a while, Fiona. But I trust him, and the doctor says—"

"Forget the doctor. And forget Aaron. He won't lie to you, but he won't know how well he actually is. People never do. But *you* might."

"Me?"

"You. Spend a few hours with him. If you can come back and give me the same answer without having to dither over it, he can return. Deal?"

Zoe smiled, stood up. "Deal," she said.

CHAPTER FOURTEEN

Marion Baker was wearing the same grey cardigan Nina had seen her in yesterday when Tom had taken her statement. Same mess of hair, and Nina was conscious enough of the state of her own hair to understand that noticing someone else's meant it really was a mess. A yellow blouse this time. Nothing much had changed.

Certainly not her mood.

"I don't know why I'm here," she said.

"It's just a voluntary interview," Nina reminded her. "You don't have to be here, Marion."

"Mrs Baker."

"You don't have to be here, Mrs Baker. We did explain that at the time."

Marion Baker sniffed. "Can't be seen not doing my duty, can I?"

"You take the lead on this one," Tom had told her. "I'll do the same for Stu Cosby."

Nina had thought she was getting the better end of the deal. Now, she wasn't so sure.

"When you spoke to my colleague yesterday," she said, gesturing to Tom beside her, "you said you weren't surprised Izzie Hopkirk had made someone angry enough to kill her. Do you mind expanding on that, Mrs Baker?"

Another sniff. "She was a horrible person. That's all. People didn't like her because she wasn't nice."

"Did you like her, Mrs Baker?"

A pause. "No. I absolutely did not."

"And apart from your general view that Izzie Hopkirk was, as you put it, a horrible person, was there anything specific that might have caused you to dislike her?"

"Oh, yes, there was." Marion Baker was sitting back with her arms folded.

"And do you mind telling us what that was?"

"That woman got me fired."

Nina felt Tom shift beside her, leaning forward. Things were getting interesting.

"Do you mind telling us a little more about that?"

Marion Baker nodded, slowly. "Oh, I don't mind at all. We worked together, you see. Workington Forestry Products. She's still there, as far as I know."

Marion Baker paused, took in the look on Nina's face, and corrected herself.

"*Was* still there, then. Izzie's... She wasn't bad at her job. But she wasn't good. And I was, and Izzie didn't like that."

"In what way?"

"In what way was she not as good as me? Well, we were both on the logistics side. Izzie made mistakes, I didn't. And of course, when that sort of thing happens, people tend to look for blame elsewhere instead of looking inside themselves. She told the managers that I was a bully."

CHAPTER FOURTEEN

"I hope you don't mind me asking, Mrs Baker, but was there any truth in the allegation?"

Another sniff. "Absolutely not. And I'd have made my case, only she managed to persuade her fellow incompetents to back her up."

"What do you mean?" asked Nina. Tom still hadn't said a word.

"Other colleagues. The ones who weren't very good. They claimed I'd bullied them, too. I was summoned to see management and told that if I left without a fuss, I'd get four weeks' pay and an adequate reference. That was how they described it. 'Adequate.' After twenty years. I will never forgive that woman."

Tom finally spoke.

"So would it be fair to say that you hated Izzie Hopkirk?"

Marion Baker frowned. Had he pushed too far, too soon?

"I think so, yes," she said. "I wouldn't have killed her, though. I don't blame whoever did, of course. But I'm not a violent woman. And I'm not stupid."

"Do you mind if we take a short break?" Nina asked. The woman nodded. The frown still hadn't left her face.

Outside Interview Room Four, it took less than a minute for Nina and Tom to agree: it was time to caution Marion Baker.

Back inside the room, Marion Baker listened quietly while they explained what was happening, and reminded her that she could ask for a lawyer and wasn't under arrest. She was perfectly entitled to leave, if she wanted.

"In that case," she said, "I'll be off. Goodbye."

She stood and walked out without another word.

CHAPTER FIFTEEN

Aaron had been awake since half past five.

There was no need for it. With luck, Annabel wouldn't wake for an hour or so, now that she was past waking seven or eight times each night. Serge had a job, but not until nearly lunchtime. There was nothing to stop him staying in bed with his husband for most of the morning.

Except that, however much he loved this, there was an itch. A need to get out there and do something, to exercise his brain and figure out how someone had done something, and why, and then, maybe, who that someone was.

It wasn't like he'd dreamed he'd become a police officer. But it had become more than just a decent job. It was a vital part of his life. And much as he loved his husband and his daughter – so much for that hour, he could hear her stirring now, calling out for a hug and something to eat – he loved his work, too. The team. The variety. The challenge.

He needed to be back there.

He heard footsteps upstairs. Serge would be checking on her. He'd be down shortly, worrying that he'd woken without

CHAPTER FIFTEEN

Aaron by his side, relieved to see him up and about and looking normal. Aaron took two steps towards the kitchen and his phone rang.

He checked the display. The boss.

"Aaron," she said. He could hear Serge coming down the stairs, calling his name. He moved into the hallway, phone pressed to his ear, and gave his husband a thumbs-up and a big smile. Serge smiled back and moved past him into the kitchen, brushing his arm with a hand as he passed.

"Boss. What's up? Murder going OK?"

Murder going OK. The things you said in this job.

"Slowly. I'm leaving the legwork to Nina and Tom."

"They'll do you proud, boss."

"They'd better," she replied. "About what you said, yesterday."

"Yes?"

"I've spoken to the super. She says it's up to me."

His heart rose. He waited.

"I need to be sure, Aaron."

"The doc's said—"

"I know what Dr Filey's said. I've read her report. More back-covering than a politician's memoirs. But I get the gist. I want to spend some time with you before I make the call, though."

"Spend some time?"

"How are you set for today?" she asked. "It's all very well talking on the phone, Aaron, but I think I've spent enough time with you to be able to tell when you're yourself and when you're not, and I need to see you face to face."

"What do you want me to do?"

"I thought maybe we could take a road trip," she said.

He bit his lip. Last time they'd taken a road trip, it had

been a lot more than just two people in a car passing the time. It had been scoping out the Port of Workington, scoping out each other, too, getting a feel for how trustworthy the other person was. Drip-feeding secrets, and watching the ripples to see how they landed.

"A road trip?" he repeated. "Where did you have in mind?"

"I don't know," she said, and he relaxed his jaw. "It's the person I want to see, not the places. We could go to Elterwater, maybe. That's where you're from, isn't it?"

"It is, boss. Lovely area, too. Have you been before?"

"I haven't."

But...

"The thing is, boss, I've got Annabel today. Serge is out this afternoon and it's not one of her nursery days."

"That's fine," the boss replied. "Bring her along."

"Really?"

"Really. This isn't work. Not police work, anyway. I want to see what state you're in. Annabel shouldn't make that any harder."

"No, boss," he said. "But if you want me to prove I'm relaxed and calm, there's something else I'll need."

"Yes?"

"I'll need to do the driving, boss."

He waited.

She sighed. "Fair enough."

He was a careful driver, a patient driver, and he knew how much it irritated her.

He grinned to himself as they set a time and ended the call. Annabel, Aaron's Volvo, Aaron behind the wheel. By the time they were done today, it would probably be the boss making an appointment with Dr Filey.

CHAPTER SIXTEEN

Cosby was an arse. No doubt about it. But unlike Marion Baker, he seemed to have enough self-awareness to realise he was an arse, and do something about it.

For starters, he hadn't walked out.

"Are you sure you hadn't come across Izzie Hopkirk before yesterday?" Tom asked.

Cosby shrugged. "Sure? No. I might have seen her somewhere. But I *am* sure I don't remember her. And she was quite memorable, wasn't she?"

Tom hadn't seen her, not alive or dead. Just photos, and people looked even more lifeless in photos than they did in the mortuary. He'd have to take Cosby's word for it.

"A number of witnesses have said that you were unhappy with her performance yesterday," he said.

Cosby blinked and scratched at his chin.

"No point denying it, is there?" He smiled with a shrug. "Yes. I was... I made certain comments that, in the cold light of day, I regret."

"Why do you regret them? Is it because Izzie's dead and you're worried that casts suspicion on you?"

Tom sensed movement beside him, Nina sitting straighter, turning towards him. She'd be wearing her warning look. Cosby hadn't been cautioned. If they went any further down this route, and actually found anything out, it wouldn't be admissible.

Be he knew that.

"Look," said Cosby, "I'm not an idiot. I might come across like an idiot, but I'm not really that person. After yesterday, I'd have been embarrassed to see her in the street. I'd like to say I'd have apologised, but I doubt I'd have had the balls for that. Excuse my language. Neither the balls, nor the humility."

He spoke softly and clearly, and Tom couldn't help contrasting that with the clips he'd seen of Stu Cosby online, performing at previous iterations of the World's Biggest Liar. On stage, he was a man of the North, an accent so thick you could plaster walls with it, words and phrases you didn't hear outside the old folks' pubs.

But it was all an act.

"Go on," said Tom.

"I'd had a couple of drinks yesterday. More than a couple. I need a few to get into character. And then... Well, your boss was there, wasn't she?"

Tom agreed.

"She'll have told you. It didn't go well. My act. I got offstage and I'd downed a pint before I took my seat in the function room. Another one while Izzie did her bit. I got annoyed. She was... Christ. She was better than me. I could see it. Everyone could see it. I acted like I didn't like her because she was a woman, but the truth was, I didn't like her being so much better than me."

Nina leaned forward. "So you don't object to women competing in the competition?"

"If I had my way, it would be open to men aged between fifty-nine and sixty-one, living within two miles of the Bridge Inn, with beer bellies, bald patches, and fourteen-year-old Subarus. Anything to keep the competition down."

Cosby shrugged. Tom wasn't entirely sure he was joking.

"So it's not women I object to. It's anything that makes it harder for me to win."

"Old boys' club," Nina muttered.

Cosby shrugged again. "It's who I am, Detective. I wish I could be someone else, but those are my opinions, and I'm too long in the tooth to change them."

CHAPTER SEVENTEEN

Upstairs, Nina outlined what they'd learned from the morning's first interview while the boss listened.

"OK," she said. "So Marion needs looking into. What about Cosby?"

Nina looked at Tom.

"Stu Cosby is an arse, boss," said Tom. "But I don't think he's a murderer."

"Nina?"

"Agreed, boss."

"Fine. Tom, you send him home." Tom left the room. "Nina, find out what you can about Marion Baker. We don't want to call her back in if we're just wasting time."

"On it, boss."

Within five minutes Nina was talking to Carol Rashid, a colleague at Workington Forestry who insisted she'd been Izzie's 'best friend in the world'.

Not a good enough friend to have actually come to see her perform on stage, Nina thought, but said nothing.

CHAPTER SEVENTEEN

"I still can't believe she's gone," Carol said. "I don't understand how something like this could happen."

"Did Izzie have any enemies that you know of?"

Carol produced an explosive scoffing noise. "Enemies? Izzie? Everyone loved her. That's what's so ridiculous. I can't... Do you think maybe it was mistaken identity?"

Izzie had announced who she was on stage in front of almost every potential suspect. If it was mistaken identity, the killer would have had a very short memory.

"So, no one that would have wished ill of her?" Nina asked. "No one at the company?"

"Everyone loved her," Carol repeated.

"No one who *used* to work there?" Nina added.

"Oh. You're talking about Marion Baker, aren't you?"

Bullseye.

"What can you tell me about Marion Baker, Carol?"

"I... I'm not sure about this, Inspector."

Nina didn't correct her. Why had this woman, so full of words, suddenly dried up?

"Why?" she asked. "What's wrong?"

"That woman. Marion Baker. She's... She threatens to sue people. I'm not sure I should say anything. I don't know what she'll do."

"This is between us, Carol. What can you tell me about her?"

"I... I didn't like her, Inspector. She was a bully. But I think you should speak to Eliott."

"Eliott?" Nina repeated, but the line was already dead.

No. Not dead. Ringing. Carol Rashid had put her through to another line.

"Eliott Stone," said a voice. High-pitched, nervous-sounding.

"Hello," said Nina, and explained who she was and why she was calling, which was made harder by the fact that she had no idea who Eliott was.

He laughed. "Marion had that effect on people," he said, and then, more sombre, "I still can't believe it about Izzie. Of all the people."

Just like Carol Rashid. It wasn't the murder that was a surprise. It was the identity of the victim. How many murder victims did they think cropped up in an average month?

Eliott, it emerged, was the head of the department Izzie and Marion had worked for. Carol still did.

"I'm the one who fired Marion. I've got it all on file. Official records. So I'm not so worried about being sued. If she was going to do that, she'd have done it already."

"What can you tell me about her, Mr Stone?"

"Just Eliott, please. She was a nasty piece of work, DC Kapoor. A bully."

"How?"

"Verbal. Constant insults directed at her colleagues, but we even had complaints from customers and suppliers. She'd mock people, and when they asked her not to, she told them to toughen up. Told them life was tough and they were acting like babies."

"Why, though?"

"Search me. By the time the file got to me, she'd reduced several colleagues to tears. She insisted it was all nonsense. Blamed Izzie, even though it wasn't Izzie who'd started the complaint. No one in the office took Marion's side, though. Whatever she's told you about Izzie Hopkirk, take it from me, it wasn't true."

Nina thanked him, and spent a minute going through it all with the boss while Tom chased forensics. The PM would

CHAPTER SEVENTEEN

be taking place later in the afternoon, apparently. And prints should come in before that.

"Let's call Marion Baker back in," said the boss. "If she won't come willingly, we can talk about an arrest. In the meantime, stress that it'll be in her best interests to come voluntarily."

"Got it, boss," Nina replied, just as her phone rang. She listened for a moment, then turned to Tom and the boss.

"Nat Hopkirk's here," she said.

"Good. You two can speak to him, right?"

Nina frowned. "I thought..."

The boss was looking at her phone and shaking her head.

"Call me if you need to," she said. "I've got places to be."

CHAPTER EIGHTEEN

"Best behaviour, OK?" Aaron said, turning to the back seat.

Annabel nodded, her expression grave, as the boss opened the passenger door and climbed in.

"Hello, Annabel," she said, leaning over to shake the girl's hand.

"Hello, DI Finch," Annabel replied.

They'd met before, of course. But there was no way Annabel could have remembered. Serge must have said something to her before they'd left, something that had made the boss's name stick in her mind.

"I'm very well, thank you," the boss replied. "How are you?"

"Bored," Annabel said. "Daddy Aaron drives too slow."

Aaron bit back his reply. Glancing to his side, he saw the boss stifling a laugh. Serge might get brownie points for reminding Annabel of the boss's name, but he'd be losing a lot more for that little comment.

CHAPTER EIGHTEEN

"Come on." He pulled out of the car park and began to head east.

The road bent north towards Cockermouth, taking them past Lamplugh. Bernard Dearborn had lived near here. The victim in a previous murder case.

A little further along, they passed the sign for Mosser. Thackthwaite. Fellbarrow. This was where Neil Colvin had met his end, stabbed to death by the same man who'd gone on to kill Huz. Who'd nearly killed Aaron.

Everywhere in this place was marked by murder, it seemed.

But Aaron was ok with it. The hills were still hills. The lakes were still lakes. The tractor in front was still doing twenty.

"Aaron," said the boss, breaking a long silence rippled only by the sound of Annabel singing quietly to herself.

"Boss?"

"Think you might consider passing the little tractor?"

"Of course, boss." He grinned, and pulled out.

They skirted Bassenthwaite and passed by Skiddaw, looming above them just a couple of hundred feet lower than Scafell itself, then headed south from Keswick.

The green here was somehow greener, he thought. Further from the sea, less scoured by the salt in the wind. He was probably imagining it.

"This really is lovely," said the boss. Aaron glanced over to see that she was looking out of the window, taking in the views of the fells between small gaps in the trees alongside the road.

There was something about the boss that didn't sit right in Cumbria. Some part of her that would never love the place the way other people did.

But that was fine.

"So," she asked, turning to look at Annabel, then back to Aaron. "Can we talk?"

He nodded. "She won't follow what we're saying."

"Tell me, then. You're sure you're OK?"

He considered.

"No," he said, finally. "I *think* I'm OK. I won't know until... No, forget that, boss. I'll never know. The same way Nina was affected by what that bastard Mick Halfpenny did to her, and Tom with Alice Winstanley, and you with—"

"David Randle and the rest of the corrupt bastards," she said.

He slowed in surprise, his foot rising from the gas, before he realised what was going on and pushed back down.

He'd been about to refer to Dean Somerville, not Randle. The boss didn't really talk about her past, about Randle, who'd gone into the Protected Persons Programme. About the others who'd been on the take down there. But he knew it affected every decision she made.

"But the point is," he continued, "I'm feeling good. Better. You know all of it, boss. More than anyone except Dr Filey. More than Serge does, really. You know when it started."

"Victor Parlick," she said.

He nodded, and slowed. Deliberately, this time.

"Elterwater," he announced.

This time, when she exclaimed at the beauty of the place, he thought maybe it was genuine.

You couldn't fail to be impressed, though. The old stone walls and the old stone houses, the gentle hills, the shimmer of water in the distance, the forests and the crags.

"Victor," he agreed as he stopped the car at a wider

stretch of road. He opened the door, breathing in the air. Different air, again. Livestock, and trees, and grass, and stone. "You know I blamed myself for that. And maybe if I hadn't got involved—"

"Don't do this, Aaron." The boss was standing beside him, outside the car, looking up at the sky.

He turned to her. "No, boss. It's OK. If I hadn't got involved, Victor might have died a hundred different ways. Or he might have lived. If I'd got to Topper sooner, Huz would still be alive, but if I'd got to him later, Adebola Taiwo would be dead, and maybe more. You do what you can, you learn from your mistakes, you move on."

"You move on," she agreed.

"Come on." He opened the back door and reached inside for Annabel. "Let's take a little walk."

CHAPTER NINETEEN

Nat Hopkirk looked like a man who'd drunk more in one night than Tom thought he'd drunk in the last twelve months.

But then, Nat Hopkirk had been through more in the last twenty-four hours than Tom had in a lifetime.

They'd sat him down in Interview Room Four, the same one where they'd spoken to Stu Cosby and Marion Baker. She'd be in again, later.

And that reminded Tom of something they hadn't raised with her.

"Mr Hopkirk." He leaned back in his chair and the man turned his weary gaze towards him.

Christ.

Tom had seen him the previous day. His world had fallen apart, and it had been there in his posture, his eyes, the way he shook, the way he spoke. But he'd been somehow *neat*.

He wasn't neat now.

"Yeah," said Nat Hopkirk.

"Do you know a woman called Marion Baker?"

Nat squeezed his eyes shut. For a moment, Tom thought

he might have fallen asleep, but then he opened them and gently shook his head.

"Don't think so."

"Used to work with your wife. Early fifties, wears cardigans."

Nat nodded. "Yeah, I remember. Big hair. They didn't get on. She had it in for Izzie, and Izzie, well..." He smiled weakly. "She didn't take well to bullies." A pause. "She wasn't there, was she?"

"There?"

"Yesterday. The pub. She wasn't..." He sat forward, his eyes wider. "She was there? Is it her? She hated my Izzie. Was she there?"

Tom glanced over at Nina. She'd be thinking the same thing Tom was thinking.

Nat Hopkirk had seen Marion Baker. They'd grunted at each other. Not friendly, but not hostile, either.

He knew she'd been there. So why was he pretending otherwise now?

Why was Nat Hopkirk lying?

"Can we take a minute, Mr Hopkirk?" he asked. "Do you mind waiting here?"

CHAPTER TWENTY

Outside Interview Room Four, Nina listened as Tom outlined his suspicions.

"Is that all?" she asked. "He saw the woman there yesterday, when he was already half-drunk and trying to come to terms with the fact that his wife had died, and he doesn't remember it now?"

Tom shrugged.

"I know it doesn't seem like much, but he wasn't drunk when he saw her. Not yet. And... I don't know. It just seems odd. Like he's trying to cover something up. Like maybe they have something going on between them he doesn't want us to know about."

She resisted a laugh. "Nat Hopkirk and Marion Baker?"

It seemed ridiculous. Nat was a good-looking man. Out of Marion Baker's league.

"I've seen stranger," Tom pointed out.

Nina nodded. She had, too.

And the surprise he'd shown, the eagerness with which he'd seized on the mention of Marion...

CHAPTER TWENTY

Was it all fake?

They'd all but dismissed Nat Hopkirk as a suspect. He was only there for what he might be able to tell them about other people, and why they might have wanted to kill his wife.

Bugger.

"We're going to have to caution him, aren't we?" she said.

Tom grinned, his expression glum. "He's not going to like it."

"We don't have much choice. And Marion's coming back in anyway. If we tell Nat we'll be speaking to her again, suggest she might be willing to give her side of the story, maybe he'll spill the beans."

"If there's any beans to spill."

For all their concerns, Nat didn't seem to mind being cautioned, and wasn't interested in having a lawyer.

"Tell me about your relationship with Marion Baker," Tom said.

Nat frowned. "I haven't seen her in ages. Don't really know her."

"You're sure of that?" asked Nina.

He turned to her and nodded, muttering a quiet *yes* when she asked him to speak for the benefit of the recording.

Nina was tired of the gentle approach. "So you weren't having an affair with Marion Baker?"

"What?" squawked Nat Hopkirk.

"Marion Baker," she repeated. "Were you having an affair with her?"

"Marion Baker? And me? An affair?"

His voice was an octave higher, his eyes wide, his mouth hanging open in disbelief between words. If he was acting, he was doing it well.

"Look," he said, a moment later. "Leaving aside the fact that I don't like the woman and I don't find her even remotely attractive, you can check my records."

"Records?"

"Where I've been the last few months. Offshore. I'm hardly ever on the mainland. I wouldn't have had time for an affair even if I'd wanted one, and I didn't want one. I loved Izzie."

He fell silent, and Nina felt Tom's eyes boring into her. They'd go through Nat's records, but they didn't need to. He hadn't been seeing Marion Baker. This had been the wrong approach from the start.

"I'm sorry," she said. "It's just... You acted, earlier, as if you hadn't seen her."

"I hadn't," said Nat, frowning. "I didn't."

"But you did, Mr Hopkirk," Tom cut in. "You acknowledged each other. Yesterday, in the bar."

"I did?" Nat seemed surprised. "We did?"

"You did."

Nat sat back and spread out his arms. "I don't know, then. Maybe I did. I was in shock. I'd just..."

His eyes filled with tears.

"It's OK, Mr Hopkirk," Nina said. "We're truly sorry. We'll... I think we can terminate this interview now. Unless you've got anything else you think we might benefit from knowing?"

Nat shook his head. "Not really. Just that Marion Baker. She really hated Izzie. I can't think of people actually wanting to kill her, but if anyone did want to, it would have been Marion."

Nina wound down the interview, and as they stood to leave, Tom's phone rang.

CHAPTER TWENTY

"Caroline," he said.

Nina turned to Nat. "Our forensics team. Hopefully, they'll have something for us."

"Hopefully," Nat replied.

Was it her imagination, or had his smile just tightened a fraction?

CHAPTER TWENTY-ONE

Carl nodded as DS Denise Gaskill ran through the latest analysis on arrests and seizures.

Since he'd joined PSD, more and more of the intelligence they used came from computers. Not just what they found on their suspects' hard drives, but complex equations that tore apart thousands of pages of apparently meaningless statistics and rearranged them into something that told a story.

On the simplest level, that meant that when they had the same number of drugs arrests as in the past, but the amount of drugs confiscated was down, then someone, somewhere, was probably dipping into the product. It got more complex when looking for patterns around other sorts of crime, but the data was still there, and Denise seemed to be getting to grips with it.

"I like it," he told her. "Run it by the DCI."

Carl ran the team, officially, but if they wanted extra resource, it had to be approved by DCI Branthwaite. Luckily, Branthwaite trusted his people.

CHAPTER TWENTY-ONE

"Already have," Denise told him. "But over here, there's something else that seems a little out of place."

Carl was struggling to focus. Row after row of numbers scrolled down the screen. He blinked, and she was showing him a graph. All this data. Was he getting too old for it?

It probably had more to do with the beer he'd drunk last night. It wasn't every day he found out he was buying a new house.

A little out of place.

He blinked again, and saw a man standing by a gate.

"The correlation seems to be strongest towards the end of each week," Denise said. "That might indicate a pattern, but it could be coincidence."

Nat Hopkirk, standing by his own gate, peering over. Why was Carl seeing that?

"The confidence level isn't high enough to go in," Denise continued, "but it might be worth looking into."

"Stop a second, Denise," he said. "I've got to make a call."

He staggered as he stood. It had been a while since he'd been this hungover. He made his way from the team room to his office, sat down, and closed his eyes.

Nat Hopkirk by the gate. Nat Hopkirk by the front door.

Sighing in relief.

Bursting into tears.

He picked up his phone, and Zoe answered on the second ring.

"Carl," she said. "Feeling any better?"

"Not really," he admitted. What was that he could hear in the background? Was it…

"Is that a sheep?"

"Loads of them. I'm out round Elterwater with Aaron."

Elterwater? What was she doing there?

It didn't matter.

"Give him my best," he said. "Listen, I've been thinking. About Nat Hopkirk."

"Poor man."

"Yeah. But when I dropped him home, the very first thing he did was go to the back gate and look into the garden. As if he was expecting to see something there."

"Right," said Zoe, and then, a beat later, "Oh. *Right*."

"And then it took him a while to get the front door open, and I might be wrong here, but when he got the key in the lock and it turned, his first reaction, before he started crying, seemed to be relief."

"So you're saying he seemed unsure about whether the locks had been changed and whether there would be a model of the Beast of Cumbria in the garden?"

Carl rubbed his forehead. "Exactly. Unsure enough to check."

"The poor man was in shock, Carl. His wife had just died."

"True," Carl conceded.

"And he'd just knocked back a hell of a lot of whisky, too," she pointed out.

In the background, he heard a child's voice. Was that singing?

"True," he repeated. "But it just seemed like an odd reaction. His wife had just died. The tears, I get. But everything else?"

It *was* singing. Here he was, stuck in a dark office looking at data with his head pounding, and Zoe was out in the sunshine listening to the bleat of lambs and a child singing.

"Maybe," Zoe didn't sound convinced.

"I'm sure it's nothing," he said. "But if any part of Nat Hopkirk believed what Izzie said on that stage was true..."

CHAPTER TWENTY-TWO

Nat's hired BMW was at the far end of the car park. Nina walked part of the way with him, nodding as he spoke. Tom couldn't make out the words; he was a few steps behind, listening to Caroline on the phone.

"Nothing clear on her body as yet," she said.

"No prints?"

"Nothing we can use. The boss, when she was checking for signs of life. The lad who found the body, Alan Miller. And Nathan Hopkirk, obviously."

"Obviously," agreed Tom.

"There might be DNA. But there were so many people around. Anyone could have brushed up against her when she was alive. In that function room. You never know, though."

"Thanks," he said, as another car drove in and parked across two spaces.

Marion Baker climbed out, scowling at the world. She'd announced that she was bringing a lawyer with her and wouldn't say a word until that lawyer arrived. She hadn't deigned to tell them which lawyer it would be, but odds were, Stan Basham's electric Audi would be sliding silently into the car park any moment now. Basham had a habit of turning up with the most difficult suspects, and making them even harder to get anything useful out of.

"Obviously, there's plenty on the furniture."

Marion Baker had spotted Nat now, and stopped. The two of them registered each other's presence, and there it was again. A tilt of the head, and an accompanying grunt.

Not outwardly hostile. But if he had to describe that little exchange, it would have been 'mutual dislike'.

So Nat Hopkirk had been telling the truth.

"Go on," said Tom to Caroline.

"Well, there's the desk, the chairs, even the mirror. I managed to pull some hairs from the floor, too, but they could have been there a while."

There were some jobs he envied, but there were plenty that filled Tom with horror. He couldn't do what Caroline Deane did on a daily basis.

"Have you pulled anything useful?" he asked.

"We're still working through it. The door handle's interesting, though."

"Door handle?"

"The one to the dressing room."

"Hasn't that got hundreds of prints on it?"

Nat had reached his car. Nina was saying goodbye. Nat turned and gave Tom a little wave. Tom waved back.

"Normally yes," Caroline said. "But as luck would have it, they polished it the morning of the event."

"Still, got to be lots there."

"A dozen or so. We've got a handful of the competitors, and a few others who agreed to provide theirs yesterday because they'd been close to the scene. Izzie herself, of course."

"Of course," Tom agreed.

"And Nathan, from when he rushed in."

Tom hadn't seen it, but he'd heard all about it: Nat Hopkirk, charging through the place like a bull until he had his wife's body in his hands. It must have been...

"Hang on," he said.

"Why?"

"Did you just say Nathan? Nathan Hopkirk?"

"Yes."

His phone was beeping. Whoever it was, they could wait.

"But the door was open, wasn't it?" he said.

Silence. The beeping had stopped.

"Nat wouldn't have needed to touch the handle to get in," he continued. He gripped the phone tighter. "I was in that corridor. You'd already sealed the door handle up by then, hadn't you?"

When Caroline replied, her voice was quiet.

"I catalogued every action. Let me see."

He waited while she pulled up her files.

"Yes. There. You're right."

"I am?"

"You are. 'Seal applied to door handle'," she read. "Seventeen minutes before Nathan Hopkirk came in."

CHAPTER TWENTY-THREE

Aaron was taking a different route back.

"Not as pretty," he told Zoe, "but there's a better signal this way."

Which was handy, as Zoe very much needed to speak to Nina or Tom.

Tom's line was busy. She waited for him to cut off whoever he was talking to and answer, but he didn't.

It wasn't like Tom to ignore a call from Zoe. Annabel was singing the theme tune to a children's TV programme as Zoe tried Nina's number instead.

"Boss?"

"Nina. Have you got Nat Hopkirk there with you?"

"And we'll dance all night, and you can dance, too," came the voice from the back seat.

"What was that, boss?" asked Nina.

"Bit quieter please, Annabel," said Aaron, but Annabel didn't seem to have heard. Zoe raised her voice and repeated herself.

"Is Nat Hopkirk still there?"

"No," Nina replied. Zoe could hear wind in the background, the sound of engines. "He's just left. Why?"

"Because," Zoe began, then stopped as Annabel launched into a rendition of 'The Wheels on the Bus' and Aaron tried frantically to quiet her.

"Hang on," said Zoe.

She pointed to the side of the road. Aaron slowed and pulled over. There were signs here for the quarry, and more signs for construction vehicles.

Conway Developments. Another Sinead Conway project. That woman was everywhere.

Zoe climbed out of the car. Beyond the sound of the wind and the bleating of sheep, she could hear the distant noise of heavy machinery.

"Nina, I've just heard from Carl. He dropped Nat home yesterday."

"Right."

"And apparently the first thing he did was check the back garden."

"Right."

"As if he wanted to be sure there wasn't a model of the Beast of Cumbria in it," Zoe continued.

There was a short silence.

"The Beast of Cumbria?" Nina said.

"That's right."

"Like, that mythical giant cat that some nutters claim to have actually seen?"

"I..." Zoe frowned. What was the Beast of Cumbria?

She'd never heard of it before Izzie's monologue.

"I don't know. But the thing is, that was the point of Izzie's story. She said she'd spent all their money on a metal model of the thing and put it in the back garden. And then she'd shacked up with the bloke who made it and changed the locks. And Carl says, after Nat had checked the back garden, he took a while to open the door and seemed relieved when his keys worked."

"Oh," Nina said. "So you're thinking he might have heard that, thought it was true, and killed her?"

"I know it sounds ridiculous, but—"

"Hang on, boss. Tom's got some news about the prints."

Tom came on the line. "Boss," he said, "Nat Hopkirk's prints were on the door handle. To the room where Izzie was killed."

Zoe drew in a breath. "I used a handkerchief. But he would have been there after me. When he—"

"No, boss," Tom interrupted. "The handle was sealed off. By the time Nathan ran through from the bar, it was—"

"Bring him back in," Zoe said. "If he won't come, arrest him."

CHAPTER TWENTY-FOUR

Stan Basham. Every bloody time. Always there. And always with the same advice.

"What did you think when you heard Izzie speaking at the Bridge Inn yesterday?" asked Tom.

"No comment," said Nat.

They'd sent Marion Baker home before her lawyer had even turned up. But Basham had hung around anyway, and it had taken him all of thirty seconds to worm himself in with Nat Hopkirk. Now he was whispering in the man's ear, telling him what he told every client.

Don't say anything.

"Before yesterday, had you ever been to the Bridge Inn?" asked Nina.

"No comment."

"Because my understanding is that you claim not to have done," she continued. "You've never been to Santon Bridge at all. Which is surprising, because your fingerprints have shown up where they had no right to be."

"No comment."

"Last time I checked, DC Kapoor," interjected Basham. "It wasn't a criminal offence to forget that you'd been to a pub before." His usual tactic of ignoring the more junior officer in the room had been thrown into chaos, given two DCs were conducting the interview. For one reason or another, he'd picked Tom to ignore and decided to speak to Nina. "Of course, I might have the law wrong on this," he added, with a smile.

Smile away. Your client's not getting away with this one.

"You arrived late, didn't you?" asked Tom.

"No comment."

"And you'd never been to the place before?" said Nina. They were alternating the questions now, making him look from one of them to the other every few seconds.

"No comment."

"And you hadn't seen your wife for, what, three months?" asked Tom.

"No comment."

"And yet, your prints ended up on Izzie's body." Nina this time.

"I went in there," said Nat. "I couldn't bear it. Just hearing... Not seeing her. I went in there and saw her and I had to hold her. You saw it." He stared at Nina.

She nodded. *Got you.*

"I did," she agreed. "You're absolutely right. And I suppose that accounts for your prints being on the door handle of the same room, doesn't it?"

Nat nodded.

"For the recording, please."

"Yes, it does."

"Because you opened the door to get to her, so you could see her one last time, yes?"

"Yes."

Basham was whispering again, but Nat Hopkirk was shaking his head. He thought he was in the clear.

"Only," Tom pointed out, "that's not actually possible, is it?"

"What?" said Nat.

"It's not possible," Nina explained, "because the door was open."

"My client could still have touched it on his way in," said Basham.

"That's perfectly possible," agreed Tom. "Only the handle had been covered by then, hadn't it?"

Nat frowned. "Covered?"

"Covered," repeated Nina. "There's a contemporaneous record of every action that took place. It shows that the handle was sealed seventeen minutes before you came into the room, by one of the crime scene team."

Nat said nothing.

"It must be a mistake," said Basham.

"Mistakes can be made," agreed Tom.

"But we've requested bodycam footage from the police and crime scene staff in the room," added Nina. "That should tell us what actually happened, shouldn't it?"

"Shit," said Nat.

"Keep quiet," snapped Basham.

"Fuck it," said Nat. "I did it."

"It?" asked Tom.

"I killed her. I wish I hadn't, but I killed her."

"Shut up," said Basham.

Nat ignored him. "I turned up late. I walked in, and there's all these people. I didn't know what it was. Some kind of show. I certainly didn't expect to see Izzie up there on the

CHAPTER TWENTY-FOUR

stage. But she's saying all this stuff, and... She always says I'm gullible. Says I've got no sense of humour. Maybe someone else would have realised. But I didn't."

"Didn't realise what?" asked Nina, more gently. Basham was sitting back, shaking his head.

"Didn't realise it was all a joke, or a lie. Whatever."

He stared at Nina and Tom, turned to his lawyer, then looked back across the table.

"I think... Now I think it was all supposed to be a surprise. She said to meet her at the pub. I didn't know... And there she is, laughing about how she's ruined our lives. Spent all our money. Shacked up with some welder. Changed the locks. And all these people cheering like it was a good thing. I just..."

"You thought it was real?" Tom asked.

"It didn't even occur to me that it might not be. I thought, if this is a joke, it's not one she'll be telling again."

"What did you do?" asked Nina.

Basham leaned towards Nat, but his client pushed him away.

"I just walked straight into the dressing room. I waited for her there. And then, when she walked in..."

He stopped, and his eyes filled with tears. Nina didn't think he was putting this on. It was real, all of it.

She waited.

"I strangled her. She was looking at me like she didn't understand what I was doing. I strangled her, and then I just walked straight out and went to the bar. Only, by then, the screens were working. World's Biggest Liar."

Nina nodded. "So you knew it was a lie. She hadn't meant it."

"I wasn't really sure until I got home. And then I knew I'd killed her for nothing."

The tears came, and there was nothing any of them could do to stop them.

Nina leaned back in her chair, the sense of exhilaration at cracking a case replaced by sadness. Nat's wife was dead. He'd be spending the next couple of decades in prison. And he hadn't *meant* it. Hadn't *wanted* to kill her. She could see things that way, if she wanted to.

But Nina didn't want to see them that way. He'd killed a woman. He'd killed her when he could simply have asked her a question and got an answer that made sense of it all. And the sort of man that did that...

Nat Hopkirk was still crying.

Cry me a river.

She terminated the interview and headed upstairs with Tom.

CHAPTER TWENTY-FIVE

"From no suspect to an arrest, a confession, and a charge in less than eight hours, Zoe. That's impressive by anyone's standards."

Fiona was beaming from across the desk. Zoe wasn't one to shrug off praise if she'd earned it, but this time, she wasn't sure she had.

"It wasn't really me," she said. "Nina and Tom pretty much led on this. If anyone deserves the credit, it was them."

"This isn't the first time your DCs have taken on the sort of role you'd normally associate with a more senior officer, is it?" Fiona observed, a thoughtful expression on her face.

Zoe could tell where this was going. The only surprise was that it was coming from Fiona, rather than Nina or Tom themselves.

Nina, more likely, she thought.

"Do you think," asked Fiona, "one of them might be persuaded to put themselves forward for the sergeants' exam?"

Zoe took a moment to think about it.

"Yes," she said. "And I'll have a word with them both, although I suspect only one of them will be interested."

Fiona nodded. "DC Kapoor. She's come a long way in the time you've been with us, Zoe. It's not much more than a year since she was picking fights with racist mobs. You should be proud of yourself."

"I'm proud of my team. And as for that fight, Nina was back again the next night protecting an innocent family while their building was getting firebombed."

"True, true," replied Fiona. She turned back to her screen.

"I spent some time with Aaron Keyes," Zoe said. "I think he's ready to come back."

"You think?"

"I'm sure of it."

Fiona smiled. "No dithering there."

"I really am sure."

"Very well."

Was that it? As easy as that?

The super was looking at her screen.

"Right," said Zoe, standing.

"Get the paperwork up here and I'll sign what I need to. You've done well in his absence, mind."

"We've been lucky. Nothing too complicated. We'll need him sooner or later."

"Fine. Pass on my congratulations to the team, Zoe." Fiona returned her focus to the screen.

Zoe smiled. An arrest, a confession, a charge.

And Aaron was coming back.

And the house. The house with the hot tub. In a matter of weeks, they might be in it.

Not a bad twenty-four hours, really.

CHAPTER TWENTY-FIVE

We hope you enjoyed reading *The Liar's Inn*. The story continues in Cumbria Crime book 5, *The Lake* as Zoe and her team find themselves back in the thick of murder and intrigue when a body is found in the ice at a rural beauty spot.

Rachel and Joel

Buy from book retailers or via the Rachel McLean website.

CUMBRIA CRIME BOOK 5, THE LAKE

Still reeling from the death of one colleague and a near miss for another, DI Zoe Finch could have done with a quiet winter.

But when a body is pulled from the ice at a rural beauty spot, Zoe and her team find themselves back in the thick of murder and intrigue. Who is the dead man? Why was he there? And is there a connection with a web of blackmail and corruption that spreads across the county?

Someone knows more than they're letting on, and their silence could cost more lives. But talking can be just as deadly.

Buy from book retailers or via the Rachel McLean website.

READ THE CUMBRIA CRIME SERIES

The Harbour

The Mine

The Cairn

The Barn

The Lake

The Wood

...and more to come

Buy from book retailers or via the Rachel McLean website.

ALSO BY RACHEL MCLEAN

The DI Zoe Finch Series – buy from book retailers or via the Rachel McLean website.

Deadly Wishes

Deadly Choices

Deadly Desires

Deadly Terror

Deadly Reprisal

Deadly Fallout

Deadly Christmas

Deadly Origins, the FREE Zoe Finch prequel

The Dorset Crime Series – buy from book retailers or via the Rachel McLean website.

The Corfe Castle Murders

The Clifftop Murders

The Island Murders

The Monument Murders

The Millionaire Murders

The Fossil Beach Murders

The Blue Pool Murders

The Lighthouse Murders

The Ghost Village Murders

The Poole Harbour Murders

...and more to come

The Ballard Down Murder, the FREE Dorset Crime prequel

The McBride & Tanner Series – Buy from book retailers or via the Rachel McLean website.

Blood and Money

Death and Poetry

Power and Treachery

Secrets and History

Read the London Cosy Mystery Series by Rachel McLean and Millie Ravensworth – Buy from book retailers or via the Rachel McLean website.

Death at Westminster

Death in the West End

Death at Tower Bridge

Death on the Thames

Death at St Paul's Cathedral

Death at Abbey Road

The Lyme Regis Women's Swimming Club series by Rachel McLean and Millie Ravensworth – buy from book retailers or via the Rachel McLean website.

The Lyme Regis Women's Swimming Club

A Brush with Death

...and more to come

ALSO BY JOEL HAMES

The Sam Williams Series – Buy now in ebook, paperback and audiobook

Dead North

No One Will Hear

The Cold Years

The Art of Staying Dead

Victims, a Sam Williams novella

Caged, a Sam Williams short

Printed and bound by CPI Group (UK) Ltd, Croydon, CR0 4YY
07/04/2026
02084981-0003